4/07

P
CLI

D0574413

YUBA COUNTY LIBRARY
MARYSVILLE

The
MATCH
Between the
WINDS

SHIRLEY CLIMO

Illustrated by
RONI SHEPHERD

Macmillan Publishing Company   *New York*   Collier Macmillan Canada   *Toronto*

Maxwell Macmillan International Publishing Group
New York   Oxford   Singapore   Sydney

Especially for Elizabeth
—S.C.

For Kendra, Megan, and Nicholas,
with love
—R.S.

Text copyright © 1991 by Shirley Climo · Illustrations copyright © 1991 by Roni Shepherd · All rights
reserved. No part of this book may be reproduced or transmitted in any form or by any means, electronic or mechan-
ical, including photocopying, recording, or any information storage and retrieval system, without permission in
writing from the Publisher. Macmillan Publishing Company, 866 Third Avenue, New York, NY 10022. Collier
Macmillan Canada, Inc., 1200 Eglinton Avenue East, Suite 200, Don Mills, Ontario M3C 3N1.
First edition Printed in Hong Kong.

1 2 3 4 5 6 7 8 9 10

The text of this book is set in 14½ point Plantin II Light. The illustrations are rendered in watercolor and gouache.

Library of Congress Cataloging-in-Publication Data · Climo, Shirley. The match between the winds / Shirley
Climo : illustrated by Roni Shepherd.—1st ed. p. cm.
   Summary: In the sky above Borneo, the East Wind and the West Wind engage in a contest to see which of them
can move Kodok the tree frog from his palm tree. [1. Winds—Fiction. 2. Borneo—Fiction.] I. Shepherd, Roni,
ill. II. Title.
PZ7.C62247Mat 1991 [E]—dc20   90-1785 CIP AC
I S B N   0 - 0 2 - 7 1 9 0 3 5 - 8

YUBA COUNTY LIBRARY
MARYSVILLE

On the island of Borneo, so the old grandfathers say, the trees and the sea have voices, and once even the winds spoke words. Although the East and the West winds were cousins, they did not sound alike.

The East Wind whispered. His breath scarcely ruffled
the waves or tickled the tops of the coconut palms.

The West Wind bellowed. When he spoke, the ocean
tossed and grumbled and palm trees bent and groaned.

One fine day, the West Wind wanted to stir up some mischief. He left his home in Singapore and breezed over to Borneo to pester his cousin. The East Wind was dozing, his head on a small white cloud.

"Caught you!" cried the West Wind. He whistled sharply, and the cloud burst into bits. It swirled through the air like flakes of coconut.

"Hei, Hei!" The East Wind puffed, pushing the shreds of cloud back together. "I'm trying to nap!"

"Wake up!" the West Wind declared. "Already today I've whipped up two waterspouts and a nasty squall." He swelled with pride. "And I was only passing by."

"I bring rain now and then," protested the East Wind.

"Drips and drizzles!" his cousin jeered. "You can't match me!"

"Did you come for a contest?" asked the East Wind in
dismay. He looked down at Borneo. Everything on the island
was at rest beneath the noontime sun. Even Kodok the tree
frog sat quite still, smiling, on the leaf of a coconut palm.
"I suppose," said the East Wind, sighing, "that we might try
to blow Kodok from his palm tree."

"Kodok!" The West Wind snorted. "That little green tree
frog?" He sniffed. "What a waste of breath!"

"Shaking Kodok from his leaf is harder than it seems," warned the East Wind.

"Watch me make that tree frog leap!" the West Wind boasted.

"I'm watching, Cousin," said the East Wind. He yawned and leaned upon his cloud.

The West Wind took a breath. "Whoosh!" he huffed.

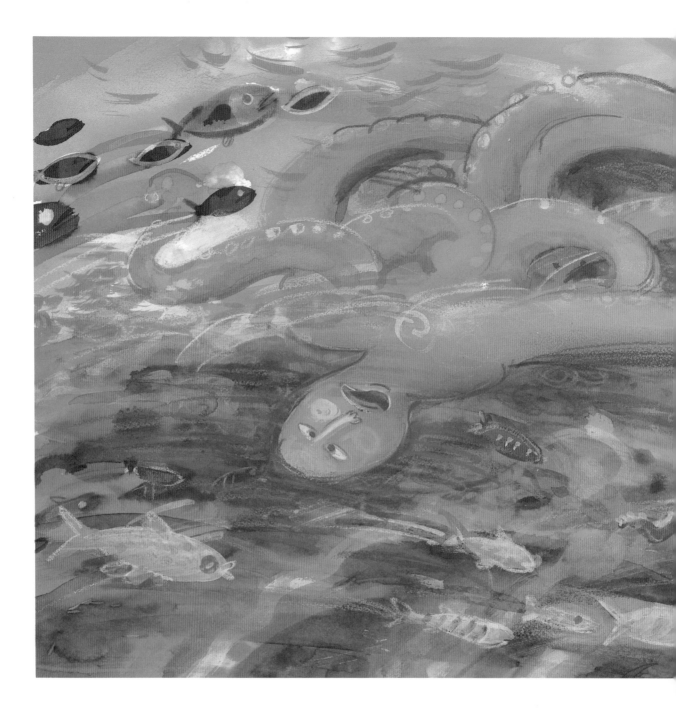

Pebbles skipped into the sea. Waves jumped against the reef and chased one another around the island.

Turtles drew in their heads, and crabs scuttled to safety under rocks.

Octopuses tangled their arms in knots, and sharks sank to the ocean floor.

Bats, hanging head down from their roosts, were flipped right-side up.

Yet...
Kodok the tree frog sat smiling on his leaf.

The West Wind scowled at Kodok. "Trickster!" he hissed.
But the East Wind answered, "Well, Cousin?"

The West Wind took a bigger breath. He bellowed louder than a thousand buffalo. Timid mouse deer stampeded deep in the jungle, and the spots on the clouded leopards shook.

The West Wind's breath flattened the people's rice paddies and lifted the thatch from the roof of their longhouse. The longhouse teetered on its tall stilt legs.

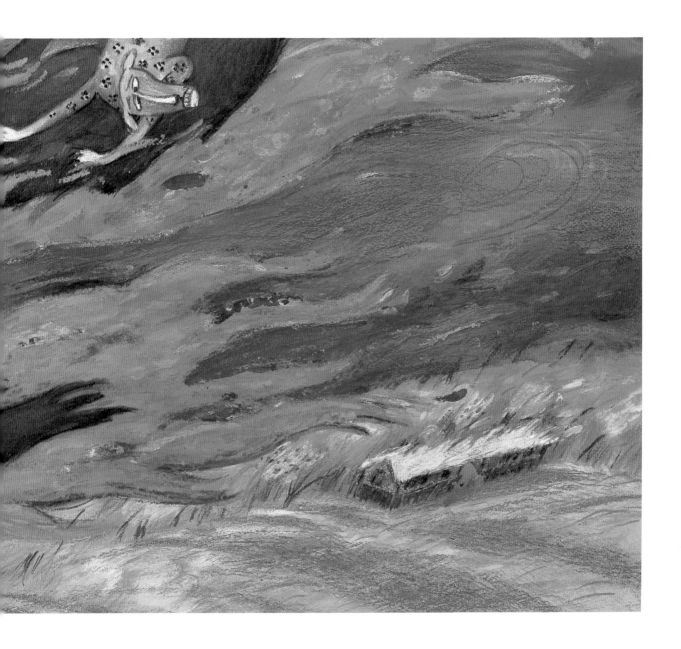

The wind plucked the feathers from the hornbills, and gold and blue and scarlet butterflies scattered like flower petals.

Pythons tied themselves around tree trunks, but monkeys were joggled loose from their vines.

Crocodiles thrashed their tails, and the bristles on the bearded pigs stood up stiff with fright.

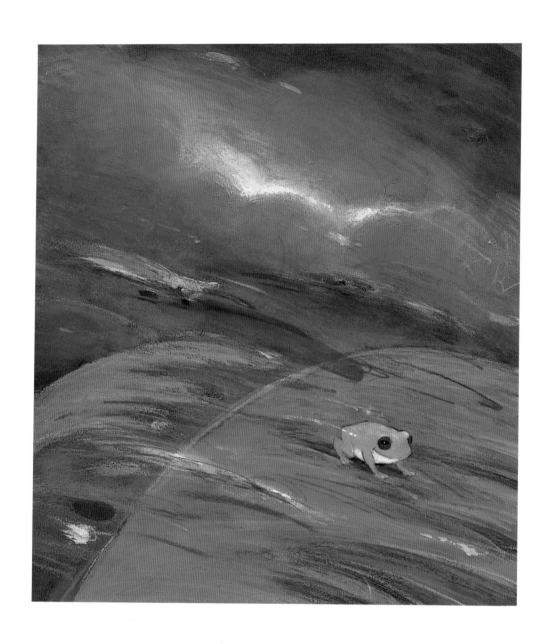

Yet...
Kodok the tree frog sat smiling on his leaf.

The West Wind was furious. "Watch out!" he shrieked at Kodok.

"Yes, Cousin?" said the East Wind.

The West Wind swallowed all the air over the island.
When he let it loose, it was a howling typhoon that made the
mountains quake.

Boulders tumbled. Bamboo trees flew about like chopsticks.
Rivers boiled over, and waterfalls streamed down the face
of Mount Kinabalu.

Seabirds were blown onto land. Land birds were blown far out to sea. The eagle fluttered like a paper kite across the ocean to Australia.

Lightning forked from the sky and singed the hair on the shaggy orangutans. The two-horned rhinoceros turned fern green with fright.

Yet ...
Kodok the tree frog sat smiling on his leaf.

The West Wind panted, rumbling louder than thunder above the coconut palm. He stretched his mouth wide, ready to gulp up Kodok.

The West Wind wheezed. He sputtered. He quivered, and his face grew purple. But he had used up his bluster. Not even a gasp was left.

"Catch your breath, Cousin," suggested the East Wind. "And watch *me*."

The East Wind began to blow. He blew so gently that
waves took off their whitecaps and fish came out of hiding.

He nudged the rain clouds from the sky. The people climbed down from their longhouse and straightened the rice stalks in the paddies.

Monkeys played tag in the trees again, and birds flew back
to their nests.

Crocodiles lazed like logs on riverbanks, and the rhinoceros wallowed in puddles until his hide was gray-brown once more.

Yet...
Kodok the tree frog sat smiling on his leaf.

Then the East Wind murmured, "Are you watching, Cousin?"

He hovered over the palm tree, and when he blew, his voice was high and thin as the hum of a mosquito. "Hush! Hush!" the East Wind sang in the tree frog's ear.

Kodok's leaf rocked in the breeze, and Kodok's head nodded. The frog pulled in his bulgy eyeballs and pulled down his eyelids. One by one, his toes loosened their hold on the leaf. Except for the East Wind's lullaby, all was quiet until...

Plop!

Kodok slipped from his leaf and settled down in the soft mud below.

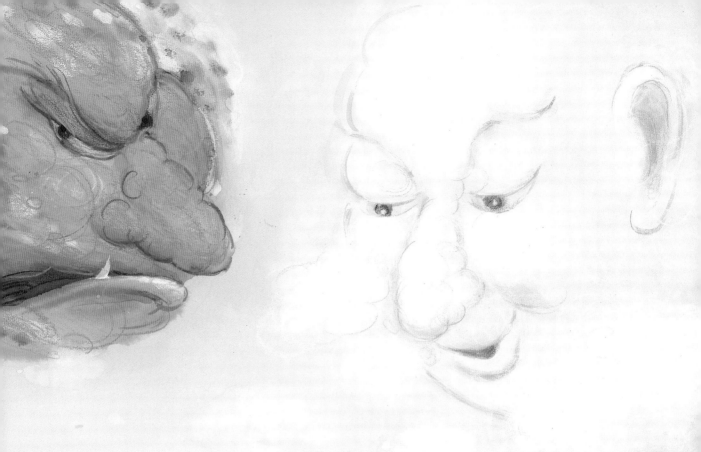

"Ssssssh!" crooned the East Wind to the tree frog. Then, raising his voice, he added, "Were you watching, Cousin?"

The West Wind was speechless. He could only moan and whine all the way home to Singapore.

But the East Wind neither heard nor saw him leave. Like Kodok the tree frog, he had drifted off to sleep.

On Borneo, when the breeze blows, the trees and the sea still whisper of the match between the winds. And that is why, so the grandfathers say, it is the East Wind who is called *Rajah Angin,* Lord of the Winds.